THE GOAT THAT ATE THE REMOTE

By Eunice Pera Hafemeister

Illustrations by Alicia Schwab

The Goat That Ate The Remote © 2024 by Eunice Pera Hafemeister. All rights reserved. No part of this book may be reproduced in any form whatsoever, by photography or xerography or by any other means, by broadcast or transmission, by translation into any kind of language, nor by recording electronically or otherwise, without permission in writing from the author's estate, except by a reviewer, who may quote brief passages in critical articles or reviews.

This is a work of fiction. Names, characters, places, and incidents are either products of the author's imagination or are used in a fictitious manner, and any resemblance to actual persons, living or dead, businesses, events, or locales is purely coincidental.

Edited by Lily Coyle
Illustrated by Alicia Schwab
Production editor: Alicia Ester

ISBN 13: 978-1-64343-977-8
Library of Congress Catalog Number: 2019903495
Printed in the United States of America

First printing: 2023
27 26 25 24 23   5 4 3 2 1

Book design and typesetting by Alicia Schwab
This book was typeset in Avenir typeface

Beaver's Pond Press
939 Seventh Street West
Saint Paul, MN 55102
(952) 829-8818
www.BeaversPondPress.com

Contact Alicia Schwab at www.aliciaschwab.com for school visits, speaking engagements, book club discussions, interviews, freelance illustration and book design projects.

Dedicated to my brothers and sisters.—E.P.H.

Dedicated to my aunt, Judy C., who loved animals and art. —A.S.

The Miller children—Tim, Sarah, and little Amy—lived in a big white house in the country.

The children loved animals and the family had lots of room for pets, including two dogs, several cats, and a woolly lamb.

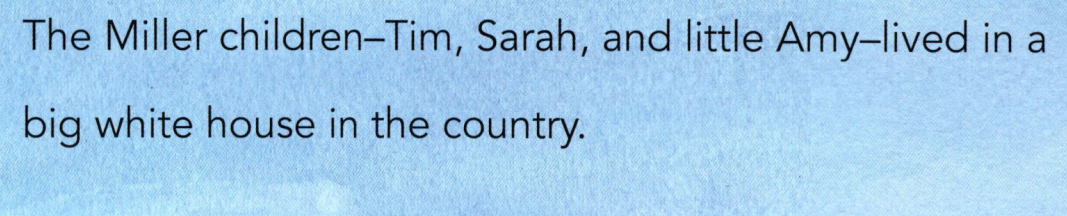

But their favorite was a sweet goat.

Gertie was little; she was brown and white and had a short tail. She was gentle and would run about and play with the children.

She was very curious and sometimes ate or chewed on things she shouldn't. Mother was not pleased when Gertie nibbled on some of her flowers.

Sometimes Gertie even ate paper! She often made the children laugh.

But on this day the children were sad because Gertie did not run and play. She was sick.

Tim and Sarah asked Mother if they could bring Gertie into the house. Mother said that they could, but Gertie must stay in a corner of the family room.

There, on a bed of straw and an old blanket she lay, sleeping much of the time. The children stretched out on the floor, watching TV. Amy was nibbling on a peanut butter sandwich. Now and then, one of the children would go to Gertie's corner to see if she was feeling better.

Soon the children became so interested in the show they were watching, they didn't notice when Gertie slowly got to her feet and wobbled across the room.

She sniffed about at some things:

Sarah's library book,

a ball,

and then the remote lying on a table.

Maybe little Amy had gotten a bit of peanut butter on the remote, because with one big gulp, Gertie swallowed it!

Then she tottered back to her bed in the corner.

Soon she began to have the hiccups.

* HIC *

When she hiccupped, the remote she swallowed changed the channels, but no one realized why!

* HIC *

* HIC *

Soon she hiccupped again, and a baseball game came on.

The children looked for the remote, hoping to go back to the show they were watching. They looked everywhere, but they could not find it.

Tim, tired of searching, began to watch the game.

But Gertie hiccupped and the channel changed again.

Mother came into the room with a stack of folded clothes in her arms.

Now there was a cooking show on, so she put down the clothes and got paper and a pencil to write down the recipe.

But as soon as she jotted a few words, Gertie hiccupped, and again the channel changed.

They all thought something must be wrong with the TV.

Since they could not watch their show, Sarah and Amy turned their attention to the goat. Gertie seemed to be feeling a little better.

While Sarah was petting Gertie, she noticed that a different show came on right when Gertie hiccupped.

* HIC *

Sarah began to wonder if Gertie's hiccups somehow affected the TV, but she couldn't imagine how.

Then Gertie stood up, her body heaving, and she gave a great cough. With that cough, out came the remote!

Now they knew the answer to the mystery!

How the children laughed. Sarah gave Gertie a hug and remarked,

"Silly Gertie! You are the goat that ate the remote."

Eunice Pera Hafemeister grew up with twelve siblings on the North Dakota prairie, where she learned about the ways of goats. She began teaching in one-room schoolhouses, and later taught Head Start for many years. She always loved reading and telling stories to children.

Besides having fun, goats can survive in challenging environments, providing nutritious milk and cheese for children and their families.

A portion of the proceeds from this book will go to donating goats to families who need them.

Alicia Schwab grew up in southern Wisconsin with a motley assortment of pets (including a toucan). She spent all her free time climbing trees, building forts, and drawing with her two siblings. She's illustrated many books, including: *The Mukluk Ball, Unicycle Dad, LITE: The High Treason Incident,* and *The Forgotten Doorway.* Learn more at: www.aliciaschwab.com